ROBERT J. BLAKE

Dog

PHILOMEL BOOKS   NEW YORK

Te moráin grá do Mhamái
For Mom, because you have great heart

Library of Congress Cataloging-in-Publication Data   Blake, Robert J.   Dog / Robert J. Blake.   p. cm.   Summary: An old man grudgingly allows a dog into his life. [1. Old age—Fiction. 2. Dogs—Fiction.] I. Title. PZ7.B564Do   1994   [E]—dc20   92-39313 CIP AC   ISBN 0-399-22019-4

1   3   5   7   9   10   8   6   4   2

First Impression

One day a dog came in from the hills. "Off with you, find yourself lost!" old Peter said. "You will get nothing but trouble from me. I've spent the whole day making this place tidy and to no one's delight. You won't be getting something for nothing here."

"Ai, it's himself here again! It will do you no good looking at me like that. I know the look of a gypsy. Stop that now! Oh now, the look again. Here, take a scrap, but then you must leave me alone."

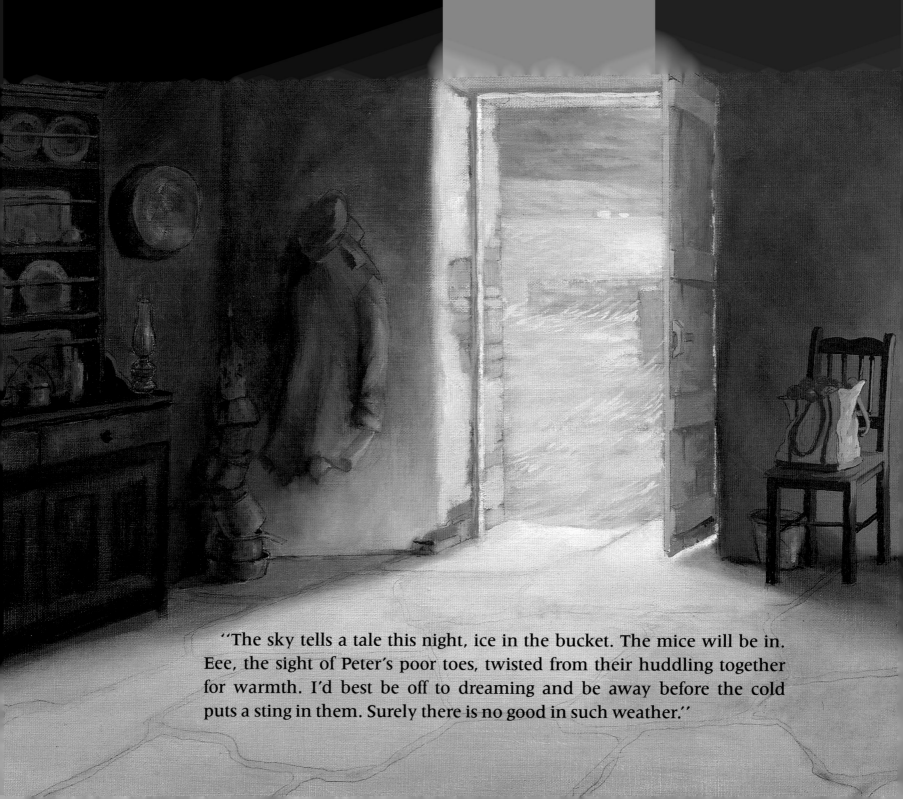

''The sky tells a tale this night, ice in the bucket. The mice will be in. Eee, the sight of Peter's poor toes, twisted from their huddling together for warmth. I'd best be off to dreaming and be away before the cold puts a sting in them. Surely there is no good in such weather.''

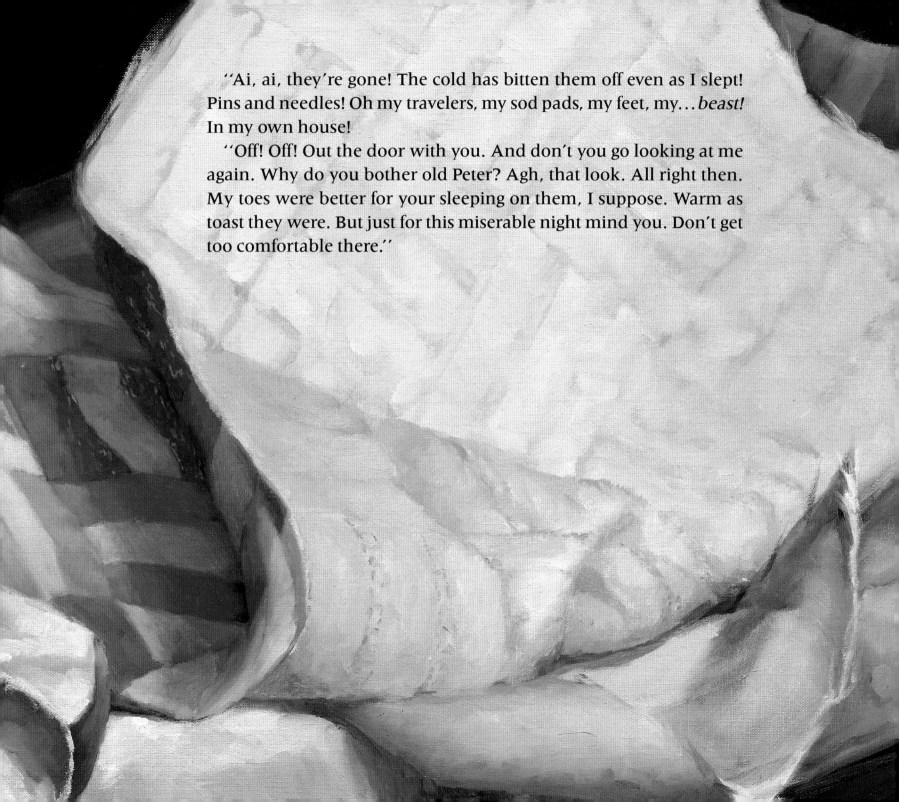

"Ai, ai, they're gone! The cold has bitten them off even as I slept! Pins and needles! Oh my travelers, my sod pads, my feet, my… *beast!* In my own house!

"Off! Off! Out the door with you. And don't you go looking at me again. Why do you bother old Peter? Agh, that look. All right then. My toes were better for your sleeping on them, I suppose. Warm as toast they were. But just for this miserable night mind you. Don't get too comfortable there.''

"Ai, ai, ai! Me giving you my own bed and it coming to this. *A dozen apples to you, and all of them rotten!*

"Out with you then, and *hard luck to you, animal! Fall in a hole!*"

"*Keep to the path there!*
 "I have no need of companions nor the trouble they bring. I have
no one to answer to and none to look after. Don't have to ask permis-
sion if I just sit wishing, and no need for the wishes I make. My own
quiet neighbors are fine company for me."

"This storm could blow a boulder over. A wise man will keep his feet to the hearth today. Agh, I hope I did not turn my fortune by putting the animal out.

"I will put out a scrap just to spare my luck. *Here then. A morsel, mongrel!* Next he'll be demanding afternoon tea. Truly, I am generous to a fault."

"Has he no sense, then? Gone most of the day and only the wind and rain to touch his food. Surely he is on the dole, begging somewhere else. *Go ahead! Warm another's feet!* And weren't my toes warm as raisins in a bun last night. Oh, he's stuck somewhere for certain, and me the one who put him out.

"All right, I will leave the door open a crack."

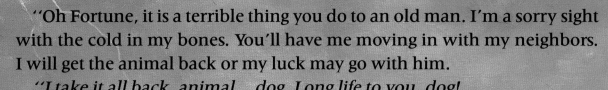

"Oh Fortune, it is a terrible thing you do to an old man. I'm a sorry sight with the cold in my bones. You'll have me moving in with my neighbors. I will get the animal back or my luck may go with him.

"*I take it all back, animal…dog. Long life to you, dog!*

"Ahhr, my fire is wanting now. I know how he feels. *We are both hungry, dog!*"

"Oh, now here is where I may find the dog. Surely, being a dog, he would go where I told him. Down a hole. I hope he has had the good sense to have no sense at all.

"*Dog. Dog? Dog!*"

"Now we are both cursed indeed. Surely you've stolen the cup from a fairy to get us into this. Don't you go looking at me. I'm cold to the marrow because of you. Don't lean on me! No licking! You'll be freezing Peter's face, now."

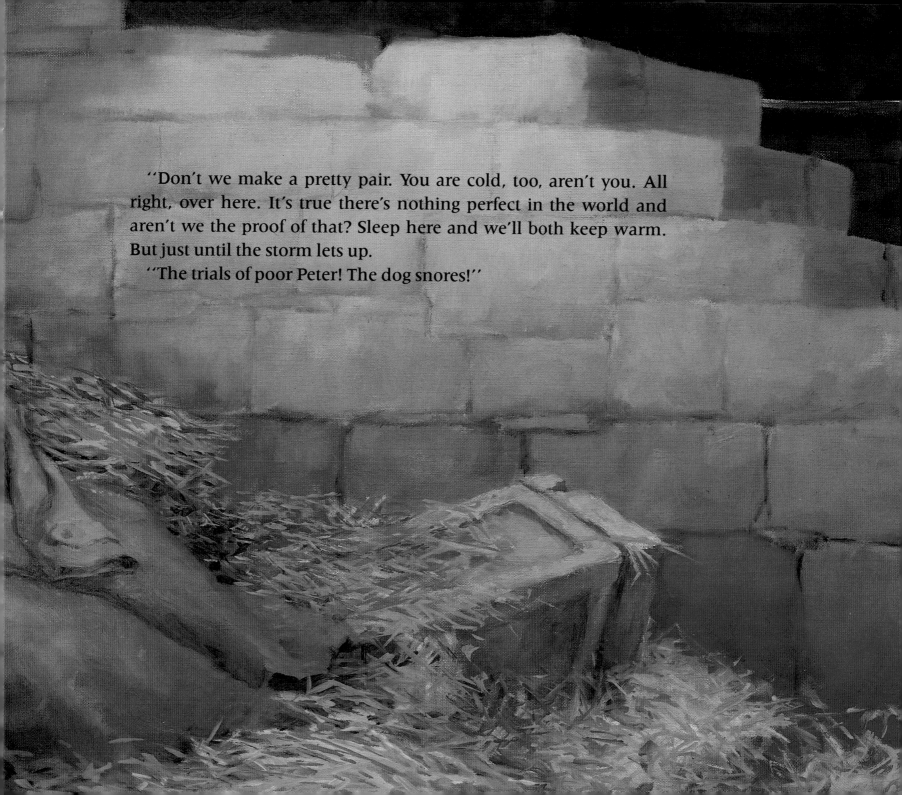

''Don't we make a pretty pair. You are cold, too, aren't you. All right, over here. It's true there's nothing perfect in the world and aren't we the proof of that? Sleep here and we'll both keep warm. But just until the storm lets up.

''The trials of poor Peter! The dog snores!''

"All right then. You are Peter's gift so surely you may stay. *Not in the house.* Well, not all the time. But don't be doing what you *must* where you shouldn't! And it will be your job to keep down the rodents. And I'll not be giving you a name! You'll know well enough who I am talking to when I speak."

"Dog."